PLANET OF SAND

PLANET OF SAND

MURRAY LEINSTER

WILDSIDE PRESS

PLANET OF SAND

CHAPTER 1

THERE WAS bright, pitiless light in the prison corridor of the *Stallifer*. There was the hum of the air renewal system. Once in every so often there was a cushioned thud as some item of the space ship's machinery operated a relay somewhere. But it is very tedious to be in a confinement cell. Stan Huckley—lieutenant, j.g., Space Guard, under charges and restraint—found it rather more than tedious. He should have been upheld, perhaps, by the fact that he was innocent of the charges made against him by Rob Torren, formerly his immediate superior officer. But the feeling of innocence did not help. He sat in his cell, holding himself still with a grim resolution. But a deep, a savage, a corrosive anger grew and grew and grew within him. It had been growing in just this manner for weeks.

The *Stallifer* bored on through space. From her ports the cosmos was not that hostile, immobile curtain of unwinking stars the early interstellar travelers knew. At twelve hundred light-speeds with the Bowdoin-Hall field collapsing forty times per second for velocity control, the stars moved visibly. Forty glimpses of the galaxy about the ship in every second made it seem that the universe were always in view. And the stars moved. The nearest ones moved swiftly and the farther ones more slowly, but all moved. From force of habit the motion gave the feeling of perspective, so that the stars appeared to be distributed in three dimensions. From the ship they seemed very small, like fireflies. All the cosmos seemed small and almost cosy. The Rim itself appeared no more than a few miles away. The *Stallifer* headed for Earth and Rhesi II. She had been days upon her journey; she had come a distance which it would stagger the imagination to compute.

In his cell, though, Stan Buckley could see only four walls. There was no variation of light; no sign of morning or night or afternoon. At intervals, a guard brought him food. That was all—except that his deep and fierce and terrible anger grew until it seemed that he would go mad with it.

He had no idea of the hour or the day when, quite suddenly, the pitiless light in the corridor dimmed. Then the door he had not seen since his entrance into the prison corridor clanked open. Footsteps came toward the cell. It was not the guard who fed him. He knew that much. It was a variation of routine, which should not have varied until his arrival on Earth.

He sat still, his hands clenched. A figure loomed outside the cell door. He looked up coldly. Then fury so great as almost to be frenzy filled him. Rob Torren looked in at him.

There was silence. Stan Buckley's muscles tensed until it seemed that the bones of his body creaked. Then Rob Torren said caustically:

"It's lucky there are bars, or there'd be no chance to talk! Either you'd kill me and be beamed for murder, or I'd kill you and Esther would think me a murderer. I've come to get you out of this if you'll accept my terms."

Stan Buckley made an inarticulate, growling noise.

"Oh, surely!" said Rob Torren. "I denounced you, and I'm the witness against you. At your trial, I'll be believed and you won't. You'll be broken and disgraced. Even Esther wouldn't marry you under such circumstances. Or maybe," he added sardonically, "maybe you wouldn't let her."

Stan Buckley licked his lips. He longed so terribly to get his hands about his enemy's throat that he could hardly hear the other's words.

"The trouble is," said Rob Torren, "that she probably wouldn't marry me, either, if you were disgraced by my means. So I offer a bargain. I'll help you to escape—I've got it all arranged—on your word of honor to fight me. A duel. To the death."

His eyes were cold. His tone was cold. His manner was almost contemptuous.

Stan Buckley said hoarsely:

"I'll fight you anywhere, under any conditions!"

"The conditions," Rob Torren told him coldly," are that I will help you to escape. You will then write a letter to Esther, saying that I did so and outlining the conditions of the duel as we agree upon them. I will, in turn, write a letter to the Space Guard brass, withdrawing my charges against you. We will fight. The survivor will destroy his own letter and make use of the other. Do you agree to that?"

"I'll agree to anything," said Stan Buckley, "that will get my hands about your throat!"

Rob Torren shrugged.

"I've turned off the guard photocells," he said. "I've a key for your cell. I'm going to let you out. I can't afford to kill you except under the conditions I named or I'll have no chance to win Esther. If you kill me under any other conditions, you'll simply be beamed as a murderer." He paused and said shortly, "And I have to come and fight you because a letter from you admitting that I've behaved honorably is the only possible thing that would satisfy Esther. You give your word to wait until you've escaped and I come for you before you try to kill me?"

Stan Buckley hesitated a long, long time. Then he said in a thick voice:

"I give my word."

Without hesitation, Rob Torren put a key in the cell door and turned it. He stood aside. Stan Buckley walked out, his hands clenched. Torren closed the door and re-locked it. He turned his back and walked down the corridor. He opened the door at its end. Again he stood aside. Stan Buckley went through. Torren closed the door, took a bit of cloth from his pocket, wiped off the key, hung it up again on a tiny hook, with the same bit of cloth threw a switch, and put the cloth back in his pocket.

"The photocells are back on," he said in a dry voice. "They say you're still in your cell. When the guard contradicts them, you'll seem to have vanished into thin air."

"I'm doing this," said Stan hoarsely, "to get a chance to kill you. Of course I've no real chance to escape!"

That was obvious. The *Stallifer* was deep in the void of interstellar space. She traveled at twelve hundred times the speed of light. Escape from the ship itself was absurd. And concealment past discovery when the ship docked was preposterous.

"That remains to be seen," said Torren coldly. "Come this way."

Down a hallway. He slipped into a narrow doorway, invisible unless one looked. Stan followed. He found himself in that narrow, compartmented space between the ship's inner and outer skins. A door, another compartment; another door. Then a tiny airlock—used for the egress of a single man to inspect or repair such exterior apparatus as the scanners for the ship's vision screens. There was a heap of assorted apparatus beside the airlock door.

"I prepared for this," said Torren. "There's a spacesuit. Put it on. Here's a meteor miner's space skid. There are supplies. I brought this stuff as luggage, in watertight cases. I'll fill the cases with my bath water and get off the ship with the same weight of luggage I had when I came on. That's my coverup."

"And I?" asked Stan harshly.

"You'll take this chrono. It's synchronized with the ship's navigating clock. At two-two even you push off from the outside of the ship. The drive field fluctuates. When it collapses, you'll be outside it. When it expands—"

Stan Buckley raised his eyebrows. This was clever! The Bowdoin-Hall field which permits of faster than speed of light travel is like a pulsating bubble expanding and contracting at rates ranging from hundreds of thousands of times per second to the forty per second of deep space speed. When the field is expanding, and bars of an artificial allotrope of carbon are acted upon by electrostatic forces in a certain particular fashion, a ship and all its contents accelerate at a rate so great that it simply has no meaning. As the field contracts, a ship decelerates again. That is the theory, at any rate. There is no proof in sensations or instrument readings that such is the case. But velocity is inversely proportional to the speed of the field's pulsations, and only in deep space does a ship dare slow the pulsations too greatly, for fear of complications.

A man in a spacesuit could detach himself from a space ship traveling by the Bowdoin-Hall field, though. He could float free at the instant of the field's collapse, and be left behind when it expanded again. But he would be left alone in illimitable emptiness.

"You'll straddle the space skid," said Torren shortly. "It's full-powered—good for some millions of miles. At two-two exactly the *Stallifer* will be as close to Khor Alpha as it will go. Khor Alpha's a dwarf white star that's used as a course marker. It has one planet that the directories say has a breathable atmosphere and list as a possible landing refuge, but which they also say is unexamined. You'll make for that planet and land. You'll make for that planet and wait for me. I'll come!"

Stan Buckley said in soft ferocity:

"I hope so!"

Torren's rage flared.

"Do you think I'm not as anxious to kill you as you are to kill me?"

For an instant the two tensed, as if for a struggle to the death there between the two skins of the space ship. Then Torren turned away.

"Get in your suit," he said. "I'll get a private flier and come after you as soon as the hearing about your disappearance is over. Push off at two-two even. Make it exact!"

He stalked away, and Stan Buckley stared after him, hating him, and then grimly turned to the apparatus on an untidy heap beside the airlock door.

Five minutes later he opened the outer door of the lock. He was clad in space armor and carried with him a small pack of supplies—the standard abandon ship kit—and the little space drive unit. The unit was one of those space skids used by meteor miners—merely a shaft which contained the drive and power unit, a seat, and a cross-shaft by which it was steered. It was absurdly like a hobby-horse for a man in a spacesuit, and it was totally unsuitable for interplanetary work because it consumed too much power when fighting gravity. For Stan, though, starting in mid-space with only one landing to make, it should be adequate.

He locked the chrono where he could see it on the steering bar. He strapped the supply kit in place. He closed the airlock door very softly, he waited, clinging to the outer skin of the ship with magnetic shoes.

The cosmos seemed very small and quite improbable. The specks of light which were suns seemed to crawl here and there. Because of their motion it was impossible to think of them as gigantic, ravening balls of unquenchable fire. They moved! To all appearances, the *Stallifer* flowed onward in a cosmos perhaps a dozen miles in diameter, in which many varicolored fireflies moved with vast deliberations.

The hand of the chrono moved, and moved, and moved. At two-two exactly, Stan pressed the drive stud. At one instant he and his improbable space steed rested firmly against a thousand-foot hill of glistening chrome steel. The waverings of the Bowdoin-Hall field were imperceptible. The cosmos was small and limited and the *Stallifer* was huge. Then the skid's drive came on. It shot away from the hull—and the ship vanished as utterly as a blown out candle flame. The universe was so vast as to produce a cringing sensation in the man who straddled an absurd small device in such emptiness, with one cold white sun—barely near enough to show a disk—and innumerable remote and indifferent stars on every hand.

On the instant the ship's field contracted and left him outside, Stan had lost the incredible velocity the field imparts. In the infinitesimal fraction of a second required for the field to finish its contraction after leaving him, the ship had traveled literally thousands of miles. In the slightly greater fraction of a second required for it to expand again, it had moved on some millions of miles. By the time Stan's mind had actually grasped the fact that he was alone in space, the ship from which he had separated himself was probably fifty or sixty millions of miles away.

He was absolutely secure against recapture, of course. If his escape went unnoticed for even half a minute, it would take all the ships of all the Space-Guard a thousand years to search the volume of space in which one small space-suited figure might be found. It was unlikely that his escape would be noticed for hours.

He was very terribly alone. A dwarf white sun glowed palely, many, many millions of miles away. Stars gazed at him incuriously, separated by light centuries of space.

He started the minute gyroscopes that enabled him to steer the skid. He started in toward the sun. He had a planet to find and land on. Of course, Rob Torren could simply have contrived his escape to emptiness so that he might die and shrivel in the void, and never, never, never through all eternity be found again. But somehow, Stan had a vast faith in the hatred which existed between the two of them.

CHAPTER 2

IT WAS TWO days later when he approached the solitary planet of Khor Alpha. The air in his spacesuit had acquired that deadly staleness which is proof that good air is more than merely a mixture of oxygen and nitrogen. He felt sluggish discomfort which comes of bottled, repurified breathing mixture. As the disk of the planet grew large, he saw little or nothing to make him feel more cheerful. The planet rotated as he drew near, and it seemed to be absolutely featureless. The terminator—the shadow line as sunlight encroached on the planet's night side—was a perfect line. There were, then, no mountains. There were no clouds. There seemed to be no vegetation. There was, though, a tiny polar icecap—so small that at first he did not discover it. It was not even a dazzling white, but a mere whitishness where a polar cap should be, as if it were hoar frost instead of ice.

He went slanting down to match the planet's ground speed in his approach. Astride the tiny space skid, he looked rather like an improbable witch astride an incredible broomstick. And he was very, very tired.

Coming up in a straight line, half the planet's disk was night. Half the day side was hidden by the planet's bulge. He actually saw no more than a quarter of the surface at this near approach, and that without magnification. Any large features would have been spotted from far away, but he had given up hope of any variation from monotony when—just as he was about to enter the atmosphere— one dark patch in the planet's uniformly dazzling white surface appeared at the very edge of day. It was at the very border of the dawn belt. He could only be sure of its existence, and   that it had sharp, specifically straight edges. He saw rectangular extensions from the main mass of it. Then he hit atmosphere, and the thin stuff thrust at him violently because of his velocity, and he blinked and automatically turned his head aside, so that he did not see the dark patch again before his descent put it below the horizon.

Even so near, no features, no natural formations appeared. There was only a vast brightness below him. He could make no guess as to his height nor—after he had slowed until the wind against his body was not detectable through the spacesuit—of his speed with relation to the ground. It was extraordinary. It occurred to him to drop something to get some idea, even if a vague one, of his altitude above the ground.

He did, an oil soaked rag from the tool kit. It went fluttering down and down—and abruptly vanished, relatively a short distance below him. It had not landed. It had been blotted out.

Tired as he was, it took him minutes to think of turning on the suit microphone which would enable him to hear sounds in this extraordinary world. But when he flicked the switch he heard a dull, droning, moaning noise which was unmistakable. Wind. Below him there was a sandstorm. He was riding just above its upper surface. He could not see the actual ground because there was an opaque wall of sand between. There might be five hundred feet between him and solidity, or five thousand, or there might be no actual solid, immovable ground at all. In any case, he could not possibly land.

He rose again and headed for the dark area he had noted. But a space skid is not intended for use in atmosphere. Its power is great, to be sure, when its power unit is filled. But Stan had come a very long way indeed since his departure from the *Stallifer*. And his drive had blown a fuse, once, which cost him power. Unquestionably, the blown fuse had been caused by the impinging of a Bowdoin-Hall field upon the skid. Some other space ship that the *Stallifer*, using Khor Alpha as a course guide, had flashed past the one planet system at many hundred times the speed of light. The pulsations of its drive field had struck the skid and drained its drive of power, and unquestionably had registered the surge. But it was not likely that it would be linked with Stan's disappearance. The other ship might be headed for a star system which was light centuries from Earth, and a minute—relatively minute—joggle of its meters would not be a cause for comment. The real seriousness of the affair was that the skid had drained power before its fuse blew.

That property of a Bowdoin-Hall field, incidentally—its trick of draining power from any drive unit in its range—is the reason that hampers its use save in deep space. Liners have to be elaborately equipped with fuses lest in shorting each other's drive they wreck their own. In interplanetary work, fuses are not even practical because they might be blown a hundred times in a single voyage. Within solar systems high frequency pulsations are used, so that no short can last more than the hundred-thousandth of a second, in which not even allotropic graphite can be ruined.

Stan, then, was desperately short of power and had to use it in a gravitational field which was prodigally wasteful of it. He had to rise high above the sandstorm before he saw the black area again at the planet's very rim. He headed for it in the straightest of straight lines. As he drove, the power gauge needle flickered steadily over toward zero. A meteor miner does not often use as much as one earth gravity acceleration, and Stan had to use that much merely to stay aloft. The black area, too, was all of a hundred-odd miles away, and after some millions of miles of space travel, the skid was hard put to make it.

He dived for the black thing as it drew near, and on his approach it appeared simply impossible. It was a maze, a grid, of rectangular girders upholding a seemingly infinite number of monstrous dead-black slabs. There was a single layer of those slabs, supported by innumerable spiderly slender columns. Here, in the dawnbelt, there was no wind and Stan could see clearly. Sloping down, he saw that ten-foot columns of some dark metal rose straight and uncompromising from a floor of sand to the height of three hundred feet or more. At their top was the grid and the slabs, forming a roof some thirty stories above the ground. There were no underfloors, no crossways, no structural features of any sort between the sand from which the columns rose and that queer and discontinuous roof.

Stan landed on the ground at the structure's edge. He could see streaks and bars of sky between the slabs. He looked down utterly empty aisles between the corridors and saw nothing but the columns and the roof until the shafts merged in the distance. There was utter stillness here. The sand was untroubled and undisturbed. If the structure were a shelter, it sheltered nothing. Yet it stretched for at least a hundred miles in at least one direction, as he had seen from aloft. As nearly as he could tell, there was no reason for its existence and no purpose it could serve. Yet it was not the abandoned skeleton of something no longer used. It was plainly in perfect repair. The streaks of sky to be seen between its sections were invariably exact in size and alignment. They were absolutely uniform. There was no dilapidation and no defect anywhere. The whole structure was certainly artificial and certainly purposeful, and it implied enormous resources of civilization. But there was no sign of its makers, and Stan could not even guess at the reason for its construction.

But he was too worn out to guess. On board the *Stallifer*, he'd been so sick with rage that he could not rest. On the space skid, riding in an enormous loneliness about a dwarf sun whose single planet had never been examined by men, he had to be alert. He had to find the system's one planet, and then he had to make a landing with practically no instruments. When he landed at the base of the huge grid, he examined his surroundings wearily, but with the cautious suspicion needful on an unknown world. Then he made the sort of camp the situation seemed to call for. He clamped the space skid and his supplies to his spacesuit belt, lay down hard by one of the columns, and incontinently fell asleep.

He was wakened by a horrific roaring in his earphones. He lay still for one instant. When he tried to stir, it was only with enormous difficulty that be could move his arms and legs. He felt as if he were gripped by quicksand. Then suddenly, he was wide awake. He fought himself free of clinging encumbrances. He had been half-buried in sand. He was in the center of a roaring swirling sand devil which broke upon the nearby column and built up mounds of sand and snatched them away again, and flung great masses crazily in every direction.

As the enigmatic structure had moved out of the dawn belt into the morning, howling winds had risen. All the fury of a tornado, all the stifling deadliness of a sandstorm, beat upon the base of the grid. And from what Stan had seen when he first tried to land, this was evidently the normal daily weather of this world. If this were a sample merely of morning winds, by mid-day existence should be impossible. Stan looked at the chrono. He had slept less than three hours. He made a loop of line from the abandon ship kit and got it about the nearest pillar. He drew himself to that tall column. He tried to find a lee side, but there was none. The wind direction changed continually. He debated struggling further under the shelter of the monstrous roof. He stared up, estimatingly—

He saw slabs tilt. In a giant section whose limits he could not determine, he saw the rectangular sections of the roof revolve in strict unison. From a position parallel to the ground, they turned until the light of the sky shone down unhindered. Vast masses of sand descended—deposited on the slabs by the wind, and now dumped down about the columns' bases. Then wind struck anew with a concentrated virulence, and the space between the columns became filled with a whirling giant eddy that blotted out everything. It was a monster whirlwind that spun crazily in its place for minutes, and then roared out to the open again. In its violence it picked Stan up bodily, with the skid and abandon ship kit still clamped to his spacesuit. But for the rope about the column he would have been swept away and tossed insanely into the smother of sand that reached to the horizon.

After a long time, he managed to take up some of the slack of the rope; to bind himself and his possessions more closely to the column which rose into the smother overhead. Later still, he was able to take up more. In an hour, he was bound tightly to the pillar and was no longer flung to and fro by the wind. Then he dozed off again. It was uneasy slumber. It gave him little rest. Once a swirling sand devil gouged away the sand beneath him so that he and his gear hung an unguessable distance above solidity, perhaps no more than a yard or so, but perhaps much more. Later he woke to find the sand piling up swiftly about him, so that he had to loosen his rope and climb wearily as tons of fine, abrasive stuff—it would have been strangling had he needed to breathe it direct—were flung upon him. But he did sleep from time to time.

Then night fell. The winds died down from hurricane intensity to no more than gale force. Then to mere frantic gusts. Then—the sun had set on the farther side of the huge structure to which he had tied himself—then there was a period when a fine whitish mist seemed to obscure all the stars. It gradually faded, and he realized that it contained particles of so fine a dust that it hung in the air long after the heavier stuff had settled.

He released himself from the rope about the pillar. He stood, a tiny figure beside the gargantuan columns of black metal which rose toward the stars. The stars themselves shone down brightly, brittly, through utterly clear air. There were no traces of cloud formation following the storm of the day. It was obvious that this was actually the normal weather of this planet. By day, horrific winds and hurricanes. By night, a vast stillness. The small size and indistinctness of the icecap he had seen was assurance that there was nowhere on the planet any sizable body of water to moderate the weather. With such storms, inhabitants were unthinkable. Life of any sort was out of the question. But if there were anything certain in the cosmos, it was that the structure at whose base he stood was artificial!

He flicked on his suit radio. Static only. Sand particles in dry air, clashing against each other, would develop changes to produce just the monstrous hissing sounds his earphones gave off. He flicked off the radio and opened his face plate. Cold dry air filled his lungs.

There were no inhabitants. There could not be any. But there was this colossal artifact of unguessable purpose. There was no life on this planet, but early during today's storm—and he suspected at other times when he could neither see nor hear—huge areas of the roof plates had turned together to dump down their accumulated loads of sand. As he breathed in the first breaths of cold air, he heard a roaring somewhere within the forest of pillars. At a guess, it was another dumping of sand from the roof. It stopped. Another roaring, somewhere else. Yet another. Section by section, area by area, the sand that had piled on the roof at the top of the iron columns was dumped down between the columns' bases.

Stan flicked on the tiny instrument lights and looked at the motor of the space skid. The needle was against the pin at zero. He considered, and shrugged. Rob Torren would come presently to fight him to the death. But it would take the *Stallifer* ten days or longer to reach Earth, then three or four days for the microscopic examination of every part of the vast ship in grim search for him. Then there'd be an inquiry. It might last a week or two weeks or longer. The finding would be given after deliberation which might produce still another delay of a week or even a month. Rob Torren would not be free to leave Earth before then. And then it would take him days to obtain a space yacht and—because a yacht would be slower than the *Stallifer*—two weeks or so to get back here. Three months in all perhaps. Stan's food wouldn't last that long. His water supply wouldn't last nearly as long at that. If he could get up to the icecap there would be water, and on the edge of the ice he could plant some of the painstakingly developed artificial plants whose seeds were part of every abandon ship kit. They could live and produce food under almost any set of planetary conditions. But he couldn't reach the polar cap without power the skid didn't have.

He straddled the little device. He pointed it upward. He rose sluggishly. The absurd little vehicle wabbled crazily. Up, and up, and up toward the uncaring stars. The high thin columns of steel seemed to keep pace with him. The roof of this preposterous shed loomed slowly nearer, but the power of the skid was almost gone. He was ten feet below the crest when diminishing power no longer gave thrust enough to rise. He would hover here for seconds, and then drift back down again to the sand, for good.

He flung his kit of food. Upward. It sailed over the sharp edge of the roof and landed there. The skid was thrust down by the force of the throw, but it had less weight to lift. It bounced upward, soared above the roof, and just as its thrust dwindled again, Stan landed it.

He found—nothing.

To be exact, he found the columns were joined by massive girders of steel fastening them in a colossal open grid. Upon those girders which ran in a line due north and south—reckoning the place of sunset to be west—huge flat plates of metal were slung, having bearings which permitted them to be rotated at the will of whatever unthinkable constructor had devised them. There were small bulges which might contain motors for the turning. There was absolutely nothing but the framework and the plates and the sand some three hundred feet below.

There was no indication of the purpose of the plates or the girders or the whole construction. There was no sign of any person or creature using or operating the slabs. It appeared that the grid was simply a monotonous, featureless, insanely tedious construction which it would have taxed the resources of Earth to build—it stretched far, far beyond the horizon—but did nothing and had no purpose save to gather sand on its upper surfaces and from time to time dump that sand down to the ground. It did not make sense.

Stan had a more immediate problem than the purpose of the grid, though. He was three hundred feet above ground. He was short of food and hopelessly short of water. When day come again, this place would be the center of a hurricane of blown sand. On the ground, lashed to a metal column, he had been badly buffeted about even in his spacesuit. Up here the wind would be much stronger. It was not likely that any possible lashings would hold him against such a storm. He could probably get back to the ground, of course, but there seemed no particular point to it.

As he debated, there came a thin, shrill whistling overhead. It came from the far south, and passed overhead, descending, and—going down in pitch—it died away to the northward. The lowering of its pitch indicated that it was slowing. The sound was remarkably like that of a small spacecraft entering atmosphere incompletely under control, which was unthinkable, of course, on the solitary unnamed planet of Khor Alpha. Stan felt very, very lonely on a huge plate of iron thirty stories above the ground, on an alien planet under unfriendly stars, and with this cryptic engineering monstrosity breaking away to sheer desert on one side and extending uncounted miles in all others. He flicked on his suit radio, without hope.

There came the loud, hissing static. Then under and through it came the humming carrier wave of a low power transmitter sending on emergency power.

"Help call! Help call! Space yacht *Erebus* grounded on planet of Khor Alpha, main drive burned out, landed in darkness, outside conditions unknown. If anyone hears, p-please answer! M-my landing drive smashed when I hit ground, too! Help call! Help call! Space yacht *Erebus* grounded on planet of Khor Alpha, main drive burned out, landed in darkness—"

Stan Buckley had no power. He could not move from this spot. The *Erebus* had grounded somewhere in the desert which covered all the planet but this one structure. When dawn came, the sandstorm would begin again. With its main drive burned out, its landing drive smashed—when the morrow's storms began it would be strange indeed if the whirlwinds did not scoop away sand from about the one solid object they'd encounter, so that the little craft would topple down and down and ultimately be covered over; buried under perhaps hundreds of feet of smothering stuff.

He knew the *Erebus*. Of course. It belonged to Esther Hume. The voice from it was Esther's, the girl he was to have married, if Rob Torron hadn't made charges disgracing him utterly. Tomorrow she would be buried alive in the helpless little yacht, while he was unable to lift a finger to her aid.

CHAPTER 3

HE WAS TALKING to her desperately when there was a vast, labored tumult to the west. It was the product of ten thousand creakings. He turned, and in the starlight he saw great flat plates—they were fifty feet by a hundred and more—turning slowly. An area a mile square changed its appearance. Each of the flat plates in a hundred rows of fifty plates had turned sidewise, to dump its load of settled sand. A square mile of plates turned edges to the sky, and turned back again. Creakings and groanings filled the air, together with the soft roaring noise of the falling sand. A pause. Another great section of a mile each way performed the same senseless motion. Pure desperation made Stan say sharply;

"Esther! Cut off for half an hour! I'll call back! I see the slimmest possible chance, and I've got to take it! Half an hour, understand?"

He heard her unsteady assent. He scrambled fiercely to the nearest of the huge plates. It was, of course, insane to think of such a thing. The plates had no purpose save to gather loads of sand and then to turn and dump them. But there were swellings at one end of each plate—where the girders to which they clung united to form this preposterous elevated grid. Those swellings might be motors. He dragged a small cutting torch from the tool kit. He snapped its end. A tiny, savage, blue-white flame appeared in mid-air half an inch from the torch's metal tip.

He turned that flame upon the rounded swelling at the end of a monster slab. Something made the slabs turn. By reason, it should be a motor. The swellings might be housing for motors. He made a cut across such a swelling.

At the first touch of the flame something smoked luridly and frizzled before the metal grew white-hot and flowed aside before the flame. There had been a coating on the iron. Even as he cut, Stan realized that the columns and the plates were merely iron. But the sandblast of the daily storms should erode the thickest of iron away in a matter of weeks, at most. So the grid was coated with a tough, elastic stuff—a plastic of some sort—which was not abraded by the wind. It did not scratch because it was not hard. It yielded, and bounced sand particles away instead of resisting them. It would outwear iron, in the daily sandblast, by a million times, on the principle by which land vehicles on Earth use rubber tires instead of metal for greater wear.

He cut away a flap of metal from the swelling. He tossed it away with his space-gloved hands. His suit flash illuminated the hollow within. There was a motor inside, and it was remarkably familiar, though not a motor such as men made for the purpose of turning things. There was a shaft. There were four slabs of something that looked like graphite, rounded to fit the shaft. That was all. No coils. No armature. No signs of magnets. Man use this same principle, but for a vastly different purpose. Men used the reactive thrust of allotropic graphite against an electric current in their space ships. The Bowdoin-Hall field made such a thrust incredibly efficient, and it was such graphite slabs that drove the *Stallifer*—though these were monsters weighing a quarter of a ton apiece, impossible for the skid to lift. Insulated cables led to the slabs in wholly familiar fashion. The four cables joined to two and vanished in the seemingly solid girders which formed all the monster grid.

Almost without hope, Stan slashed through two cables with his torch. He dragged out the recharging cable of the skid. He clipped the two ends to the two cut cables. They sparked! Then he stared. The meter of the skid showed current flowing into its power bank. An amazing amount of current. In minutes, the power storage needle stirred from its pin. In a quarter of an hour it showed half charge. Then a creaking began all around.

Stan leaped back to one of the cross girders just as all the plates in an area a mile square about him began to turn. All but the one whose motor housing he had cut through. All the other plates turned so that their edges pointed to the stars. The sand piled on them by the day storm poured down into the abyss beneath. Only the plate whose motor housing Stan had cut remained unmoving. Sparks suddenly spat in the metal hollow, as if greater voltage had been applied to stir the unmoving slab. A flaring, lurid, blue-white are burned inside the hollow. Then it cut off.

All the gigantic plates which had turned their edges skyward went creaking loudly back to their normal position, their flat sides turned to the stars. Nothing more happened. Nothing at all. In another ten minutes, the skid's meter showed that its power bank was fully charged. Stan, with plenty to think about, straddled the little object and went soaring northward like a witch on a broom, sending a call on his suit radio before him.

"Coming, Esther! Give me a directional and let's make it fast! We've got a lot to do before daylight!"

He had traveled probably fifty miles before her signal came in. Then there was a frantically anxious time until he found the small helpless space yacht, tumbled on the desert sand, with Esther peering hopefully out of the airlock as he swooped down to a clumsy landing. She was warned and ready. There was no hope of repairing the drive. A burned out drive to operate in a Bowdoin-Hall field calls for bars of allotropic graphite—graphite in a peculiar energy state as different from ordinary graphite as carbon diamond is from carbon coal. There were probably monster bars of just such stuff in the giant grid's motors, but the skid could not handle them. For tonight, certainly repair was out of the question. Esther had hooked up a tiny, low power signaling device which gave out a chirping wave every five seconds. She wore a spacesuit, had two abandon ship kits, and all the water that could be carried.

The skid took off again. It was not designed to work in a planet's gravitational field. It used too much power, and it wobbled erratically, thus for sheer safety Stan climbed high. With closed face plates the space suited figures seemed to soar amid the stars. They could speak only by radio, near as they were.

"Wh-where are we going, Stan?"

"Icecap," said Stan briefly. "North pole. There's water there—or hoar frost, anyhow. The day storms won't be so bad—if there are storms at all. In the tropics on this planet the normal weather is a typhoon-driven sandstorm. We'll settle down in the polar area and wait for Rob Torren to come for us. It may be three months or more."

"Rob Torren—"

"He helped me escape," said Stan briefly. "Tell you later. Watch ahead."

He'd had no time for emotional thinking since his landing, and particularly since the landing of the little space yacht now sealed up and abandoned to be buried under the desert sand. But he knew how Esther came to be here.

She'd had news of the charges Rob Torren had brought against him. She hadn't believed them. Not knowing of his embarcation for Earth for courtmartial—the logical thing would have been a trial at advanced base—she'd set out desperately to assure him of her faith. She couldn't get a liner direct, so she'd left alone in her little space yacht. In a sense, it should have been safe enough. Craft equipped with Bowdoin-Hall drive were all quite capable of interstellar flight. Power was certainly no problem any more, and with extra capacitors to permit low frequency pulsations of the drive field, and mapped dwarf white stars as course markers, navigation should be simple enough. The journey, as such, was possibly rash but it was not foolhardy. Only—she hadn't fused her drive when she changed its pulsation frequency. When she was driving past Khor Alpha, her Bowdoin-Hall field had struck the space skid on which Stan was trying to make this planet-and the field had drained his power. The short circuit blew the skid's fuse, but it burned out the yacht's more delicate drive. Specifically, it overloaded and ruined the allotropic carbon blocks which made the drive work. Esther's predicament was caused not only by her solicitude for Stan, but by the drive of the skid on which he'd escaped from the *Stallifer*.

He blamed himself. Bitterly, but even more he blamed Rob Torren. Hatred surged up in him again for the man who had promised to come here and fight him to the death. He said quietly:

"Rob's coming here after me. Talk about that later. He didn't guess this place would be without water and with daily hurricanes everywhere except—I hope!—the poles. He thought I'd be able to make out until he could come back. We've got to! Watch out ahead for the sunset line. We've got to follow it north until we hit the polar cap. With water and our kits we should be able to survive indefinitely."

The spacesuited figures were close together—in fact, in contact. But there was no feeling of touching each other through the insulating, almost inflexible armor of their suits. Sealed as they were in their helmets and communicating only by phone in the high stratosphere, neither could feel the situation suitable for romance. Esther was silent for a time. Then she said:

"You told me you were out of power—"

"I was," he told her. "I got some from the local inhabitants—if they're local."

"What—"

He described the preposterous, meaningless structure on the desert. Thousands of square miles in extent. Cryptic and senseless and of unimaginable significance.

"Every slab has a motor to turn it. I cut into a housing and there was power there. I loaded up with it. I can't figure the thing out. There's nowhere that a civilized or any other race could live. There's nothing those slabs could be for!"

There was a thin line of sunlight far ahead. Traveling north, they drove through the night and overtook the day. They were very high indeed, now, beyond atmosphere and riding the absurd small skid that meteor miners use. They saw the dwarf white sun Khor Alpha. Its rays were very fierce. They passed over the dividing line between day and night, and far, far ahead they saw the hazy whitishness which was the polar cap of this planet.

It was half an hour before they landed, and when they touched ground they came simply to a place where wind blown sand ceased to be powdery and loose, and where there was plainly dampness underneath. The sun hung low indeed on the horizon. On the shadow side of sand hillocks there was hoar frost. All the moisture of the planet was deposited in the sand at its poles, and during the long winter nights the sand was frozen so that even during the summer season unthinkable frigidity crept out into every shadow.

Stan nodded at a patch of frost on the darker side of a half-mile sand dune.

"Sleeping," he said dryly," will be done in spacesuits. This ground will be cold where the sun doesn't hit! Do you notice that there's no sign of anything growing anywhere? Not even moss?"

"It's too cold?"

"Hardly!" said Stan. "Mosses and lichens grow on Earth as far north as the ground ever thaws. And on every other planet I've ever visited. There'd be plants here if anywhere, because there's water here. There simply can't be any life on this planet. None at all!"

Then the absurdity of the statement struck him. There was that monstrous grid, made by intelligence of some sort and using vast resources. But—

"Darn!" said Stan. "How can there be life here? How can plants live in perpetual sandstorms? How can animals live without plants to break down minerals and make them into food? How can either plants or animals live without water? If there were life anywhere, it would have to be near water, which means here. And if there's none here there can't be any life at all—"

They reached the top of the dune. Esther caught her breath. She pointed.

There, reaching across the dampened sand, was a monstrous and a horrifying trail. Something had come from the zones where the sandstorms raged. It had passed this way, moving in one direction, and it had passed again, going back toward the stormy wastes. By the trail, it had ten or twelve or twenty legs, like some unthinkable centipede. The tracks of its separate sets of legs were separated by fifteen feet. Each footprint was two yards across.

CHAPTER 4

FOR THREE days by the chrono on the space skid, the hard-white sun Khor Alpha circled the horizon without once setting. Which was natural, because this was one of the poles of Khor Alpha's only planet, and this was summer. In those three days Stan and Esther saw no living thing. No bird, beast, or insect; no plant, moss, or lichen. They had planted the seeds from their abandon ship kits, included in such kits because space castaways may have to expect to be isolated not for weeks or months, but perhaps for all their lives. The seeds would produce artificially developed plants with amazing powers of survival and adaptation and food production. On the fourth day—clock time—the first of the plants appeared above the bank of damp sand in which they had been placed. In seven days more there would be food from them. If one plant of the lot was allowed to drop its own seeds, in time there would be a small jungle of food plants on which they could live.

For the rest, they lived in a fashion lower than any savage of Earth. They had no shelter. There was no building material but sand. They slept in their spacesuits for warmth. They had no occupation save that of waiting for the plants to bear food, and after that of waiting for Rob Torren to come.

And when he came, the presence of Esther changed everything. When Torren arrived to fight a duel to the death with Stan, the stake was to have been ultimately Esther's hand. But if she were present, if she knew the true story of Torren's charges against Stan and their falsity, he could have no hope of winning her by Stan's death. He would have nothing to gain by a duel. But he would gain by the murder of one or both of them. Safety from the remotest chance of later exposure, at any rate, and revenge for the failure of his hopes. If he managed to kill Stan by any means, fair or foul, Esther would be left wholly at his mercy.

So Stan brooded, hating Rob Torren with a desperate intensity surpassing even the hatred he'd felt on the *Stallifer*. A large part of his hatred was due to helplessness. There was no way to fight back. But he tried desperately to think of one.

On the fourth day he said abruptly:

"Let's take a trip, Esther."

She looked at him in mute inquiry.

"For power," he said, "and maybe something more. We might be able to find out something. If there are inhabitants on this planet, for instance. There can't be, but there's that beast—"

Esther nodded.

"Maybe it's somehow connected with whatever or whoever built that grid, that checkerboard arrangement I told you about. Something or somebody built that, but I can't believe anything can live in those sandstorms!" said Stan.

They'd followed the huge trail that had been visible on their first landing in the polar regions. The great, two-yard-across pads of the monster had made a clear trail for ten miles past the point of their discovery. At the end of the trail there was a great gap in a cliff of frozen sand. The thing seemed to have devoured tons of ice-impacted stuff. Then it had gone back into the swirling sandy wastes. It carried away with it cubic yards—perhaps twenty or thirty tons—of water-filled frozen sand.

But reason insisted that there could be no animal life on a planet without plants, and no plants on a desert which was the scene of daily typhoons, hourly hurricanes, and with no water anywhere upon it save at the poles. There was no vegetation there. A monster with dozens of six-foot feet, and able to consume tons of wetted sand for moisture, would need vast quantities of food for energy alone. It was unthinkable that food was to be found in the strangling depths of sandstorms.

"There's another thing," Stan added. "With power to spare I could fuse sand into something like a solid. Make a house, maybe, and chairs to sit on, instead of having to wear our spacesuits all the time. Maybe we could even heat the inside of a house!"

Esther smiled at him.

"Darling," she said wrily, "you've no idea how glad I'd be of a solid floor to walk on instead of sand and a chair to sit on, even if we didn't have a roof!"

They had been, in effect, in the position of earth castaways marooned on a sand cay which had not even seashells on it or fish around it. There was literally nothing they could do but talk.

"And," she added, "if we could make a tub to take a bath in—"

She brightened at the thought. Stan hadn't told her of his own reasons for having no hope. There was no point in causing her despair in advance.

"We'll see what we see," said Stan. "Climb aboard."

The space skid was barely five feet long. It had a steering bar and a thick body which contained its power storage unit and drive. There was the seat which one straddled, and the strap to hold its passenger. Two people riding it in bulky spacesuits was much like riding double on a bicycle, but Stan would not leave Esther alone. Not since they'd seen that horrifying trail!

They rose vertically and headed south in what was almost a rocket's trajectory. Stan, quite automatically, had noted the time of sunrise at the incredible structure beside which he'd landed. Later he'd noted as automatically the length of the planet's day. So to find his original landing place he had only to follow the dawn line across the planet's surface, with due regard for the time consumed in traveling.

They were still two hundred miles out in space when he sighted the grid. He slanted down to it. It was just emerging from the deep black shadow of night. He swooped to a landing on one of the hundred foot slabs of hinged metal three hundred feet above ground. It was clear of sand. It had been dumped.

Esther stared about her, amazed.

"But—people made this, Stan!" she insisted. "If we can get in touch with them—"

"You sit there," said Stan briefly. He pointed to an intersection of the crisscrossing girders. "It takes power to travel near a planet. My power bank is half drained already. I'd better fill it up again."

He got out his cutting torch. He turned it upon a motor housing. The plastic coating frizzled and smoked. It peeled away. Metal flared white-hot and melted.

There was a monstrous creaking. All the plates in a square mile turned. Swiftly. Only a desperate leap saved Stan from a drop to the desert thirty stories below.

The great slabs pointed their edges to the sky. Stan waited. Esther said startledly.

"That was on purpose, Stan!"

"Hardly," said Stan. "They'll turn back in a minute." But they did not turn back. They stayed tilted toward the dawning sky.

"You may be right, at that," said Stan shortly. "We'll see. I'll try another place."

Five minutes later they landed on a second huge slab of black metal, miles away. Without a word, Stan ensconced Esther on the small platform formed by crossing girders. He took out the torch again. The tiny, blue-white flame. Smoke at its first touch. Metal flowed—

With a vast cachinnation of squeakings, a mile-square section shifted like the first

"Something," said Stan grimly," doesn't want us to have power. Maybe they can stop us, and maybe not."

The swelling which was the motor housing was just within reach from the immovable girder crossing on which Esther waited. Stan reached out. The torch burned with quiet fierce flame. A great section of metal fell away, exposing a motor exactly like the one he'd examined— slabs of allotropic graphite and all. He thrust in and cut the cables. He reached in with the charging clips—

There was a crackling report in the space skid's body. Smoke came out.

Stan examined the damage with grimly set features.

"Blew another fuse," he said shortly. "We're licked. When I took power the first time, I temporarily ruined a motor. It's been found out. So the plates turned, today, to—scare me away, perhaps, as soon as I cut into another. When I didn't scare and severed the cables, high-voltage current was shot into the cables to kill me or ruin whatever I was using the power for. Whether there's life here or not, there's intelligence—and a very unpleasant kind, too!"

He re-fused the skid, scowling.

"No attempt to communicate with us!" he said savagely. "They'd know somebody civilized cut into that motor housing! They'd know it was an emergency! You'd think—"

He stopped. A faint, faint humming sound became audible. It seemed to come from nowhere in particular—or from everywhere. It was not the formless humming of a rising wind, though the before-dawn twilight was already light and the sky was bright with approaching day. This sound was a humming punctuated by hurried, rhythmic clankings. It was oddly like the sound of cars traveling over an old-fashioned railway, one with unwelded rail joints. Esther jerked her head about.

"Stan! Look there!"

Something hurtled toward them in the gray dawn light. It was a machine. Even in the first instant of amazement, Stan could see what it was and what it was designed to do. It was a huge, bulbous platform above stiltlike legs. At the bottoms of the legs were wheels. The wheels ran on the cross girders as on a railroad track, and the body of the thing was upraised enough to ride well above the sidewise-tilted slabs. There were other wheels to be lowered for travel on the girders which supported the slabs. It was not a flying device, but a rolling one. It could travel in either of two directions at right angles to each other, and had been designed to run only on the great grid which ran beyond the horizon. It was undoubtedly a maintenance machine, designed to reach any spot where trouble developed, for the making of repairs, and it was of such weight that even the typhoonlike winds of a normal day on this world would not lift it from its place.

It came hurtling toward them at terrific speed. It would roll irresistably over anything on the girders which were its tracks.

"Get on!" snapped Stan. "Quick!"

Esther moved as swiftly as she could, but spacesuits are clumsy things. The little skid shot skyward only part of a second before the colossus ran furiously over the place where they had been. A hundred feet beyond, it braked and came to a seemingly enraged stop. It stood still as if watching the hovering, tiny skid with its two passengers.

"It looks disappointed," said Stan dourly. "I wonder if it wants to chase us?"

He sent the skid darting away. They landed. In seconds the vibration caused by the huge machine's motion began and grew loud. They saw it race into view. As it appeared, instantly a deafening clamor began. Slabs in all directions rose to their vertical position, so that the two humans could not dodge from one row of girders to another. Then with a roar and a rush the thing plunged toward them once more.

Again the skid took off. Again the huge machine over-ran the spot where they had been, then stopped short as if baffled. Stan sent his odd craft off at an angle. Instantly the gigantic thing was in motion, moving with lightning speed in one direction, stopping short to move on a new course at right angles to the first, and so progressing in zigzag but very swift pursuit.

"Won't you land and let me crush you, said the monster to us two," said Stan drily. "They won't let us have any more power, and we haven't any more to waste. But still—"

He listened to his suit radio, twisting the tuning dials as he sent the skid up in a spiral.

"I'm wondering," he observed, "if they're trying to tell us something by radio. And meanwhile I'd like a more comprehensive view of this damned checkerboard!"

A faint, faint, wavering whine came into the headphones.

"There's something," he commented. "Not a main communication wave, though. A stray harmonic, and of a power beam, I think. They must use plenty of short waves!"

But he was searching the deadly monotony of the grid below him as he spoke. Suddenly, he pointed. All the area below them to the horizon was filled with the geometric shapes of grid and squares. But one space was different from the rest. Four squares were thrown into one, there. As the skid dived for a nearer view, that one square was seen to be a deep, hollow shaft going down toward the very vitals of this world. As Stan looked, though, it filled swiftly with something rising from its depths. The lifting thing was a platform, and things moved about on it.

"That's that!" said Stan hardily.

He shot the skid away in level flight at topmost speed,

with the great rolling machine following helplessly and ragingly on its zigzag course below.

The horizon was bright, now, with the sunrise. As Stan lifted for the rocketlike trajectory that would take him back to the polar regions, the white sun came up fiercely. There was a narrow space on which the dawn rays smote so slantingly that the least inequality of level was marked by shadow. Gigantic sand dunes were outlined there. Beyond, where the winds began, there was only featureless swirling dust.

Stan was very silent all the way back. Only once he said shortly:

"Our power units will soak up a pretty big charge in a short time. We packed away some power before the fuse blew."

There was no comment for Esther to make. There was life on the planet. It was life which knew of their existence and presence—and had tried to kill them for the theft of some few megawatts of power. It would not be easy to make terms with the life which held other life so cheaply.

With the planet's only source of power now guarded, matters looked less bright than before. After they had reached the icecap, they slanted down out of airlessness to the spot which was their home because their seeds had been planted there. As they dived down for a landing, their real situation appeared.

There was a colossal object with many pairs of legs moving back and forth over the little space where their food plants sprouted. In days, those plants would have yielded food. They wouldn't yield food now.

Their garden was being trampled to nothingness by a multilegged machine of a size comparable to the other machine which had chased them on the grid. It was fifty feet high from ground to top, and had a round, tanklike body all of twenty feet in diameter. Round projections at one end looked like eyes. It moved on multiple legs which tramped in orderly confusion. It stamped the growing plants to pulped green stuff in the polar sand. It went over and over and over the place where the food necessary for the humans' survival had promised to grow. It stamped and stamped. It destroyed all hope of food. It destroyed all hope.

Because, as Stan drove the skid down to see the machine more closely, it stopped in its stamping. It swung about to face him, with a curiously unmachinelike ferocity. As Stan veered, it turned also. When he sped on over it and beyond, it wheeled and came galloping with surprising speed after him.

Then they saw another machine. Two more. Three. They saw dark specks here and there in the polar wastes, every one a machine like the one which had tramped their food supply out of existence. Every one changed course to parallel and approached the skid's line of travel. If they landed, the machines would close in.

There was only so much power. The skid could not stay indefinitely aloft. And anywhere that they landed—

CHAPTER 5

BUT THEY did land. They had to. It was a thousand miles away, on the dark side of the planet, in a waste of sand which looked frozen in the starlight. The instant the skid touched ground, Stan made a warning gesture and reached over to turn off Esther's suit radio. He opened his own face plate and almost gasped at the chill of the midnight air. With no clouds or water vapor to hinder it, the heat stored up by day was radiated out to the awful chill of interstellar space at a rate which brought below zero temperatures within hours of sundown. At the winter pole of the planet, the air itself must come close to turning liquid from the cold. But here, and now, Stan nodded in his helmet as Esther opened her face plate.

"No radio," he told her. "They'll hardly be able to find us in several million square miles if we don't use radio. But now you get some sleep. We're going to have a busy time, presently!"

Esther hesitated, and said desperately:

"But—who are they? What are they? Why do they want to kill us?"

"They're the local citizens," said Stan. "I was wrong, There are inhabitants. I've no more idea what they may be like than you have. But I suspect they want to kill us simply because we're strangers."

"But how could an intelligent race develop on a planet like this?" demanded Esther unbelievingly. "How'd they stay alive while they were developing?"

Stan shrugged his shoulders.

"Once you admit that a thing is so," he said drily, "you can figure out how it happened. This sun is a dwarf white star. That means that once upon a time it exploded. It flared out into a nova. Maybe there were other planets nearer to it than this, and they volatilized when their sun blew up. Everything on this planet, certainly, was killed, and for a long, long time afterward it was surely uninhabitable by any standard. There's a dwarf star in the Crab Nebula which will melt iron four light hours away, and that was a nova twelve hundred years ago. It must have been bad on this planet for a long time indeed. I'm guessing that when the first explosion came the inner planets turned to gas and this one had all its seas and forests and all its atmosphere simply blasted away to nothingness. Everything living on its surface was killed. Even bacteria in the soil turned to steam and went off into space. That would account for the absolute absence of life here now."

"But—" said Esther.

"But," said Stan, "the people—call them people—who lived here were civilized even then. They knew what was coming. If they hadn't interstellar drive, flight would do them no good. They'd have nowhere to go. So maybe they stayed. Underground. Maybe they dug themselves caves and galleries five—ten—twenty miles down. Maybe some of those galleries collapsed when the blowup came, but some of the people survived. They'd stay underground for centuries. They'd have to! It might be fifty thousand years that they stayed underground, while Khor Alpha blazed less and less fiercely, and they waited until they could come up again. There was no air for a while up here. They had to fight to keep alive, down in the planet's vitals. They made a new civilization, surrounded by rock, with no more thought of stars. They'd be hard put to it for power, too. They couldn't well use combustion, with a limited air supply. They probably learned to transform heat directly to power. You can take power—electricity—and make heat. Why not the other way about? For fifty thousand years and maybe more they had to live without even thinking of the surface of their world. But as the dwarf star cooled off, they needed its heat again."

He stopped. He seemed to listen intently. But there was no sound in the icy night. There were only bright, unwinking stars and an infinity of sand—and cold.

"So they dug up to the surface again," he went on. "Air had come back, molecule by molecule from empty space, drawn by the same gravitation that once had kept it from flying away. The fused-solid rock of the surface, baked by day and frozen by night, had cracked and broken down to powder. When air came again and winds blew, it was sand. The whole planet was desert. The people couldn't live on the surface again. They probably didn't want to. But they needed power. So they built that monster grid they're so jealous of."

"You mean," Esther demanded incredulously, "that's a generator?"

"A transformer," corrected Stan. "Solar heat to electricity. Back on earth the sun pours better than a kilowatt of energy on every square yard of Earth's surface in the tropics, over three million kilowatts to the square mile. This checkerboard arrangement is at least a hundred and fifty by two hundred miles. The power's greater here, but on earth that would mean ninety thousand million kilowatts. More than sixty thousand million horsepower, more than the whole Earth uses even now! If those big slabs convert solar radiation into power—and I charged up the skid from one of them—there's a reason for the checkerboard, and there's a reason for dumping the sand—it would hinder gathering power—and there was a reason for getting upset when somebody started to meddle with it. They're upset! They'll have the conservation of moisture down to a fine point, down below, but they made those leggy machines to haul more water from the poles. When they set them all to hunting us, they're very much disturbed! But luckily they'd never have worked out anything to fly with, underground, and they're not likely to have done so since, considering the storms and all."

There was silence. Esther said slowly:

"It's—very plausible, Stan. I believe it. They'd have no idea of space travel, so they'd have no idea of other intelligent races, and actually they'd never think of cast-aways. They wouldn't understand, and they'd try to kill us to study the problem we presented. That's their idea, no doubt. They've all the resources of a civilization that's old and scientific. They'll apply them all to get us, and they won't even think of listening to us! Stan! What can we do?"

Stan said amusedly, there in the still, frigid night of an unnamed planet:

"Why—we'll do plenty! We're barbarians by compar-ison with them, Esther, and barbarians have equipment civilized men forget. All savages have spears, but a civi-lized man doesn't even always carry a pocket knife. If we can find the *Erebus*, we can probably defy this whole planet, until they put their minds to developing weapons. But right now you go to sleep. I'll watch."

Esther looked at him dubiously. Five days of sand-storms should have buried the little yacht irrecoverably.

"If it's findable," she said. Then she added wistfully, "But it would be nice to be on the *Erebus* again. It would feel so good to walk around without a spacesuit! And—" she added firmly; "after all, Stan, we are engaged! If you think I like trying to figure out some way of getting kissed through an opened face plate—!"

Stan said gruffly:

"Go to sleep!"

He paced up and down repeatedly. They were remarkably unlike castaways in the space tale tape-dramas. In those works of fiction, the hero is always remarkably ingenious. He contrives shelters from native growths on however alien a planet he and the heroine may have been marooned on; he is full of useful odd bits of information which enable him to surprise her with unexpected luxuries, and he is inspired when it comes to signaling devices. But in five days on this planet, Stan had been able to make no use of any natural growth because there wasn't any. He'd found no small luxuries for Esther because there was literally nothing about but sand. There was strikingly little use in a fund of odd bits of information when there was only desert to apply it to—desert and sandstorms. What he'd just told Esther was a guess; the best guess he could make, and a plausible one, but still a guess. The only new bit of information he'd picked up so far was the way the local inhabitants made electric motors.

He watched the chrono, and a good half-hour before night would strike the checkerboard grid he was verifying what few preparations he could make. A little later he waked Esther, just about twenty minutes before the sunset line would reach the grid, they soared upward to seek it. If Stan's plan didn't work, they'd die. He was going to gamble their lives and the last morsel of power the skid's power unit contained, on information gained in two peeps at slab motors on the grid, and the inference that all motors on this planet would be made on the same principle. Of course, as a subsidiary gamble, he had also to bet that he in an unarmed and wrecked space yacht could defy a civilization that had lived since before Khor Alpha was a dwarf star.

They soared out of atmosphere on a trajectory that saved power but was weirdly unlike an normal way of traveling from one spot on a planet's surface to another. Beneath them lay the vast expanse of the desert, all dense, velvety black except for one blindingly bright area at its Western rim. That bright area widened as they neared it, overtaking the day. Suddenly the rectatigular edges of the grid shed appeared, breaking the sharp edge of dusk.

The *Erebus* had grounded roughly fifty miles northward from the planet's solitary structure. Stan turned on his suit radio and listened intently. There was no possible landmark. The dunes changed hourly during the day and on no two days were they ever the same. He skimmed the settling sand clouds of the dusk belt. Presently he was sure he had overshot his mark.

He circled. He circled again. He made a great logarithmic circle out from the point he considered most likely. The power meter showed the drain. He searched in the night, with no possible landmark. Sweat came out on his face.

Then he heard a tiny click. Sweat ran down his face. He worked desperately to localize the signal Esther had set to working in the yacht before she left it. When at last he landed and was sure the *Erebus* was somewhere under the starlit sand about him, he looked at the power gauge and tensed his lips. He pressed his space helmet close to Esther's, until it touched. He spoke, and his voice carried by metallic conduction without the use of radio.

"We might make it if we try now. But we're going to need a lot of power at best. I'm going to gamble the local yokels can't trace a skid drive and wait for morning, to harness the whirlwinds to do our digging for us."

Her voice came faintly back to him by the same means of communication.

"All right, Stan."

She couldn't guess his intentions, of course. They were probably insane. He said urgently:

"Listen! The yacht's buried directly under us. Maybe ten feet, maybe fifty, maybe Heaven knows how deep! There's a bare chance that if we get to it we can do something, with what I know now about the machines in use here. It's the only chance I know, and it's not a good one. It's only fair to tell you—"

"I'll try anything," said her voice in his helmet, "with you."

He swallowed. Then he stayed awake and desperately alert, his suit microphones at their highest pitch of sensitivity, during the long and deadly monotonous hours of the night.

There was no alarm. When the sky grayed to the eastward, he showed her how he hoped to reach the yacht. The drive of the skid, of course, was not a pulsatory field such as even the smallest of space yachts used. It was more nearly an adaptation of a meteor repeller beam, a simple reactive thrust against an artificial mass field. It was the first type of electronic drive ever to lift a ship from earth. For takeoff and landing and purposes like meteor mining it is still better than the pulsating-field drive by which a ship travels in huge if unfelt leaps. But in atmosphere it does produce a tremendous back blast of repelled air. It is never used on atmosphere fliers for that very reason, but Stan proposed to make capital of its drawback for his purpose.

When he'd finished his explanation, Esther was more than a little pale, but she smiled gamely.

"All right, Stan. Go ahead!"

"We'll save power if we wait for the winds," he told her.

Already, though, breezes stirred across the dawn-lit sand. Already there were hot breezes. Already the fine, impalpable sand dust which settled last nightfall was rising in curious opaque clouds which billowed and curled and blotted out the horizon. But the grid was hidden anyhow by the bulge of the planet's surface.

Stan pointed the little skid downward in a hollow he scooped out with his space-gloved hands. He set the gyros running to keep it pointed toward the buried yacht. He had Esther climb up behind him. He lashed the two of them together, and strapped down to the skid. He waited.

In ten minutes after the first sand grains pelted on his armor, the sky was hidden by the finer dust. In twenty there were great gusts which could be felt even within the spacesuits. In half an hour a monster gale blew.

Stan turned on the space skid's drive. It thrust downward toward the sand and the buried yacht. It thrust upward against the air and pelting sand.

In three-quarters of an hour the sandstorm had reached frenzied violence, but the skid pushed down from within a little hollow. Its drive thrust up a spout of air. That spout drew sand grains with it. But it was needful to increase the power. After an hour a gigantic whirlwind swept around them. It tore at the two people and the tiny machine. It sucked up such a mass of powdery sand particles that its impact on the spacesuits was like a savage blow. Emptiness opened beneath the skid and sand went whirling up in a sand spout the exact equivalent of a water spout at sea. Stan and Esther and the skid itself would have been torn away by its violence but that the skid's drive was on full, now. The absurd little traveler thrust sturdily downward. When sand was drawn away by wind, it burrowed down eagerly to make the most of its gain.

Its back thrust kept a steady, cone-shaped pressure on the sand which would have poured in upon it. Stan and Esther were buried and uncovered and buried again, but the skid fought valorously. It strove to dig deeper and to fling away the sand that would have hidden it from view. It remained, actually, at the bottom of a perpetually filling pit which it kept unfilled by a geyser of upflung sand from its drive.

In twenty minutes more another whirlwind touched the pit briefly. The skid—helped by the storm—dug deeper yet. There came other swirling maelstroms.

The nose of the skid touched solidly. It had burrowed down nearly fifty feet, with the aid of whirlwinds, and come to the yacht *Erebus*.

But it was another hour before accident and fierce efforts on Stan's part combined to let him reach the airlock door, and maneuver the skid to keep that doorway clear, and for Esther to climb in—followed by masses of slithering sand—and Stan after her.

Inside the buried yacht, Stan fumbled for lights. He made haste to turn off the signaling device that had led him back to it deep under the desert's surface. It was strangely and wonderfully still here, buried under thousands of tons of sand.

Esther slipped out of her spacesuit and smiled tremulously at Stan.

"Now—?"

"Now," said Stan," if you want to you can start cooking. We could do with a civilized meal. I'll see what I can do toward a slightly less uncertain way of life."

He went forward. The *Erebus* was a small yacht, to be sure. It was a bare sixty feet overall, and of course as a pleasurecraft it had no actual armament. But within two bulging blisters at the bow the meteor repellers were mounted. In flight, in space, they could make a two-way thrust against stray bits of celestial matter, so that if a meteor was tiny it was thrust aside, or if too large the *Erebus* swerved away. From within Stan changed the focus of the beams. They had been set to send out tiny artificial matter beams no larger than a rifle bore. At ten miles such a beam would be six inches across, and at forty a bare two feet. He adjusted both to a quickly widening cone and pointed one up, the other down. One would thrust violently against the sand under the yacht, and the other against the sand over it. The surface sand, at least, could rise and be blown away. The sand below would support the yacht against further settling.

He went back to where Esther laid out dishes.

"I've started something," he told her. "One repeller beam points up to make the sand over our heads effectively lighter so it can be blown away more easily. The storm ought to burrow right down to us, with that much help. After we're uncovered, we may, just possibly, be able to work up to the surface. But after that we've got to do something else. The repellers aren't as powerful as a drive, and it's hardly likely we could lift out of gravity on them. Even if we did, we're a few light centuries from home. To fix our interstellar drive we need the help of our friends of the grid."

Esther paused to stare.

"But they'll try to kill us!" she protested. "They've tried hard! And if they find us we've no weapons at all, not even a hand blaster!"

"To the contrary," said Stan drily, "we've probably the most ghastly weapon anybody ever invented, only it won't work on any other planet than this."

Then he grinned at her. He was out of his spacesuit too, now. The food he'd asked her to prepare was out on the table, but he ignored it. He took one step toward her. And then there came a muffled sound, picked up by the outside hull microphones. It grew in volume. It became a roar. Then the yacht shifted position. Its nose tilted upward.

"The first step," said Stan, "is accomplished. I can't stop to dine. But—"

He kissed her hungrily. Five days—six, now—in spacesuits with the girl one hopes to marry has its drawbacks. An armored arm around the hulking shoulders of another suit of armor—even with a pretty girl inside it— is not satisfying. To hold hands with three-eighth-inch space gloves is less than romantic. And to try to kiss a girl three-quarters buried in a space helmet leaves much to the imagination. Stan kissed her. It took another shifting movement of the yacht, which toppled them the length of the cabin, to make him stop.

Then he laughed and went to the control room. Vision screens were useless, of course. The little ship was still most of her length under sand, but the repellers' cones of thrust had dug a great pit down to her. Now Stan juggled the repellers to take fullest advantage of the storm. At times—with both beams pushing up—the ship was perceptibly lifted by up-rushing air. Stan could be prodigal with power, now. The skid was sharply limited in its storage of energy, but all the space between the two skins of the *Erebus* was a power bank. It could travel from one rim of the Galaxy to the other without exhausting its store. The upward lift of whirlwinds—once there were six within ten minutes—and the thrusts of the repellers gradually edged the *Erebus* to the surface.

Before nightfall, it no longer lay in a sand pit. It was only half-buried in sand. The winds died down to merely savage gales, at twilight, and then slowly diminished to more angry gusts. At long last there was calm and even the impalpable fine dust that settled last no longer floated in the air. The stars shone; Stan was ready.

He turned on the ship's communicator and sent a full power wave out into the night. He spoke. What he said would be unintelligible, of course, but he said sardonically to the empty desert under the stars:

"Yacht *Erebus* calling! Down on the desert, every drive smashed, and not so much as a hand blast on board for a weapon. Maybe you'd like to come and get us!"

Then—and only then—he went and ate the meal Esther had made ready.

It was half an hour before the microphones gave warning. Then they relayed clankings and poundings and thuddings on the sand. It was the sound of heavy machines marching toward the *Erebus*. Scores of them. The machines separated and encircled the disabled yacht, though they were invisible behind the dunes all about. Then, simultaneously, they closed in.

The landing beams of the *Erebus* flashed out. Light flickered in the chill darkness. The beams darted here and there.

Then the machines appeared. The scene was remarkable. Over the dunes marched gigantic metal monsters, many-legged, with bodies as great as the *Erebus* itself. Great bulges on their forward parts gave the look of eyes, as if these were huge insects marching to devour and destroy. As the landing light beams flickered from one to another of them, huge metallic tusks appeared, and toothed jaws—used for excavation. They were not machines designed for war, but they were terrifying, and they could be terrible.

Esther's hand on Stan's shoulder trembled as the monsters closed in. Then Stan, in the unarmed and seemingly defenseless little space yacht, swung the meteor repeller controls and literally cut them to pieces.

CHAPTER 6

"WE'RE BARBARIANS," said Stan, "compared to these folk. So we've an advantage. It's likely to be only temporary, though!"

He watched the carcasses of the great machines, flicking the landing light beams back and forth. They were tumbled terribly on the ground. Some were severed in two or three places, and their separate sections sprawled astonishedly on a dune side. One was split through lengthwise. Another had all of one set of legs cut off clean, and lay otherwise unharmed but utterly helpless.

Out of that incapacitated giant a smaller version of itself crawled. It was like a lifeboat. Stan watched. Other small versions of the great machines appeared. One made a dash at the *Erebus*, and he cut it savagely in two. There was no other attack. Instead, the smaller many-legged machines ran busily from one to another of the wrecks—seeming to gather up survivors—and then went racing away into the dark. Then there was stillness.

"They knew we saw them," said Stan grimly. "They knew we could smash them. They realized that I wouldn't unless they attacked again. I wonder what they think of us now?"

"What you did to them was—awful," said Esther. She shuddered. "I still don't know what it was. I never heard of any weapon like that!"

"It could only exist here," said Stan. He grimaced. "We've meteor repellers. They push away anything in their beam. I narrowed them to their smallest size and put full power into them. That was all."

"But meteor repellers don't cut!" protested Esther.

"These did," said Stan. "They were working through sand, just that. They pushed it. With a force of eighty tons in a half-inch beam. The sand that was in the beam was shot away with an acceleration of possibly fifty thousand gravities—and more sand kept falling into the beam. Each particle was traveling as fast as a meteor when it hit, over there. When it struck it simply flared to incandescent vapor. No atomic torch was ever hotter! And there was no end to the sand I threw. You might say I cut those machines up with a sandblast, but there was never such a sandblast as this! It took a barbarian—like me—to think of it."

He continued to watch the vision screens, filtered to view their surroundings by infrared and seeing nearly as brightly as if by day.

"Now," he added, "I need to go over to those machines and get some stuff I think they've got in them. That's what I provoked this attack for. But maybe the drivers are laying low to jump on me if I try it. I'll have to wait until nearly dawn. They won't risk waiting until almost time for the sandstorms! Not with fifty miles to travel back to the grid!"

He stayed on guard. Presently he yawned. He stood up and paced back and forth, glancing from time to time at the screen. After a long time Esther said:

"You didn't sleep last night, Stan. Could I watch for a while so you can rest?"

"Mmmmm. Yes. If anything stirs, wake me. But I don't look for action here. The real action will be back underground, where they'll put their best brains to devising weapons. They ought to make up some pretty devices, too, but if they haven't thought of such things for fifty thousand years or so it may take them a while to get started."

He went back into the cabin and threw himself down. Almost instantly he was asleep. Esther watched the vision plates dutifully. There was silence and stillness everywhere. After a long time she looked in on the sleeping Stan. A little later she looked in again, reached over, and touched his hair gently. Later still she looked in yet again. She kissed him lightly—he did not wake—and went back to the control cabin, to watch the vision plates.

Nothing happened. Bright stars shone down on the night side of the desert world, and sandstorms raged and howled and blew frenziedly on the side under the dwarf white sun. But nothing happened in or near the *Erebus*.

Out in space, though, very many millions of miles away, a tiny mote winked into existence as if by magic, with the cutting off of its Bowdoin-Hall field drive. It hung seemingly motionless for a while, as if orienting itself. It seemed to locate what it sought, and vanished, but again winked into being a bare few thousand miles from the planet's surface. It did not disappear again. It drove down toward the half-obscured disk at the normal acceleration of a landing drive. Toward dawn it screamed down into atmosphere above the planet's surface. It drove on into the day, and into howling winds and far-flung sand. It rose swiftly, and went winging toward the summer polar cap. Khor Alpha's single planet had gone unvisited by men during two centuries of interstellar travel, but now there had been three separate visitations within ten days.

The last of the three visitors settled to ground where hoar frost partly whitened the desert's face. A full power carrier wave spread out from it. In the control room of the *Erebus* a speaker suddenly barked savagely:

"Stan Buckley! I'm here to kill you! Communicate!" A pause, and the same savage words again:

"Stan Buckley! I'm here to kill you! Communicate!"

Esther gasped. She recognized the voice. Rob Torren. Back more than two months before Stan had expected him. The words did not make sense to her. Stan had tried to spare her despair by concealing the fact that Torren's return would be to kill him, under a compact which her presence here made void.

"Rob!" cried Esther softly into the transmitter. "Rob Torren. It's Esther calling! Esther Hume!"

An indescribable sound emitted from the speaker. With trembling hands she adjusted the vision receiver. She looked into the taut, drawn, raging features of Rob Torren. He stared at her out of the screen.

"Stan's asleep, Rob!" cried Esther eagerly. "He didn't expect you back for a long time yet! You're wondering how I got here? Oh—"

Laughing a little, joyously, she told of her desperate voyage to be with Stan when he should be tried, and how her drive had been burned out by impinging on the drive of the space skid on which Stan had left the *Stallifer*. Of course she told of her subsequent meeting with Stan.

"There are inhabitants here," she finished eagerly, "and they've been trying to kill us. They attacked tonight and we fought them off. Stan has some hope, I think, of getting the material to repair our drive from the machines he wrecked."

She was all joy and relief at Torren's arrival. But his face was ravaged by conflicting emotions, all of them intense and all harrowing. He did not smile. His eyes seemed to burn. The strangeness of his look struck her, suddenly.

"But—what's the matter, Rob?" she asked. "You look so queer!" Then she added in abrupt, startled doubt. "And Rob! Why did you say you had come back to kill Stan? You were joking, weren't you?"

He raged at her instantly:

"He coached you, eh? To pretend you didn't know anything? Trying to make me take you both to safety on a promise of fighting me later? It won't work! I've a line on your wave and I'll be coming! I'll be coming fast! Maybe you've no weapons, but I have! I've a Space Guard one-man ship. I forced the *Stallifer* to dock at Lora Beta and put me ashore! I got this ship to hunt back for Stan, claiming his recapture as my responsibility! I did plan to have him write you a letter before I killed him, but since you know everything now—"

She saw the beginning of an infuriated movement. Then the screen went blank.

After a moment's frightened irresolution she went to Stan. She woke him, and after the first three words he was sternly alert. He listened, though—his hands clenched—until she was through.

"This sets things up nicely!" he said bitterly. "You didn't know about him, of course, but—our friends of the grid are concocting weapons to destroy us, and now he's streaking here along his locator line to blast us with everything a Space Guard ship can carry! He'll have long range stuff! He can burn us to a crisp if we put a repeller beam on him! We can't sandblast him! We can't—"

He stopped, frowning.

"We don't know how far away he is," he snapped. "There's a margin of error in locators on a planet. It might take him just long enough to find us—"

He began to struggle swiftly into a spacesuit. Esther said quickly:

"Wherever you're going, I'm going too!"

"You're not!" he said harshly. "You'll go in the control room with your hands on the beam controls. If some of the local citizens are hiding in those wrecks, you'll smash them if they jump me! I haven't so much as a pocket knife! You've got to be my weapons while I dig into those wrecks!"

He went swiftly out the airlock with only a cutting torch in his hands. He fairly ran toward the debris of the attacking army of machines. He reached the first. It had been sliced longitudinally in half by a stream of sand particles traveling at fifty miles or better per second, in a stream of air of the same velocity. Nothing could have withstood such an attack. No material substance in the universe could have resisted it. Four-inch plates of steel and foot-thick girders had been cut through like so much dough, the severed edges turned not to liquid but to vapor by the deadly stream.

The whole mechanism of the machine was exposed. The great biting jaws, designed to tear away huge masses of intermingled sand and ice. The tusks to break loose sections for the jaws to handle. The tanks to contain the precious damp material. The machine had not been made for fighting, but it, alone, could have torn the *Erebus* to fragments. With an army of such machines—

Stan clambered into the neatly halved shell with his cutting torch. All about him were small devices; cryptic things; the strictly practical contrivances of a hundred thousand year old civilization. He itched to examine them, but he needed certain bars of allotropic graphite he suspected would be here. They were. The motors which ran the leg movements were motors like those which turned the great slabs. They consisted of slabs of graphite and the metal which slid past them. That was all. Only one special allotrope of graphite makes a motor of such simplicity. Only—

He burdened himself with black, flaky bars, cutting ruthlessly through machinery an engineer would have devoted months to study. He had an even dozen of the bars in his arms when a sudden blast rocked him. He whirled, and saw a small cloud of still incandescent vapor and something which was separating horribly into many steaming pieces. Other things seemed to leap to smother him under their weight. He could not see them save as vague shapes, but he knew they were there.

Another exploded as Esther, in the *Erebus* and watching with the infrared scanner, desperately used the weapon which had never existed before and could not be used anywhere save on this one planet.

Stan ran clumsily for the ship over the drifting, powdery sand. Inhumanly resolute unhuman things leaped after him. He saw the flares as Esther destroyed them. He knew that she was wide-eyed and trembling and sick with horror at what she had to do.

He stumbled into the airlock and dogged it shut behind him. Esther came running to greet him, not shaking and not trembling and not horrified, but with burning eyes and the fiery anger of a Valkyrie.

"They tried to kill you!" she cried fiercely. "They were hiding! They'd have murdered you—"

He put down his bars of allotropic graphite. He reached out to take her in his arms. But—

"Darn these spacesuits!" he said furiously. "You'll have to wait to be kissed until this job's finished!"

He tore up the flooring hatch above the little ship's drive. He jerked off the housing.

"Keep watch!" he called to the control room. "At least one of the machines must be waiting behind the dunes, hoping for a break!"

He worked with frantic haste, shedding his spacesuit by convulsive movements. This should have been the most finicky of fine fitting jobs. To repair a Bowdoin-Hall drive unit by replacing its graphite bars for maximum efficiency is a matter for micrometric precision. But efficiency was not what he wanted, now, but speed. The stolen bars almost fitted. They were vastly unlike the five hundred pound monsters for the grid slabs. They should at least move the ship, and if the ship could be moved—

He had two of them in place and six more to go when the speaker in the control room blared triumphantly.

"Stan Buckley! Tune in! I'm right above your ship! Tune in!"

Stan swore in a sick disgust. Two out of eight was not enough. He was helpless for lack, now, of time. The corrosive hatred that comes of helplessness filled him. He went into the control room and said drearily to Esther:

"Sorry, my dear. Another twenty minutes and you'd have been safe. I think we lose."

He kissed her, and with fury steadied fingers tuned in the communication plate. Rob Torren grinned furiously at him.

"I thought I'd let you know what's happening," said Torren in a voice that was furry with whipped-up rage. "I'm going to go back and report that you were killed resisting arrest. I'm going to melt down the yacht until it could never be identified as the *Erebus*—if anybody ever sees it again! And—maybe you'll enjoy knowing that I did the things I charged you with, and have the proceeds safely banked away! I faked the evidence that proved it on you. I hoped to have Esther, too, but she's spoiled that by trying to come and help you! Now—"

"Now," said Stan coldly, "you'll stand off a good twenty miles and beam us. You'll take no chances that we might be able to throw a handful of sand at you! You'll be so cautious that you won't even come close to see your success with your own eyes! You'll read it off on instruments! You're pretty much afraid of me!"

"Afraid?" raged Rob Torren. "You'll see!"

The communication screen went blank. Stan leaped to the meteor repeller controls and stared at the vertical vision plate which showed all the sky above.

"Not the shadow of a chance," he said coldly, "but a beam does make a little glow! if he misses us once—but he won't—maybe I can get in one blast . . ."

There was tense silence. Deadly silence. The screen overhead showed a multitude of cold, unwinking stars. One of them winked out and on again.

"I'll try—" began Stan.

Then the screen seemed to explode into light. Something flared like a nova in the sky. Intolerable brilliance filled a quarter of the screen, and faded. Swiftly. It went out.

"Wh-what was that?" chattered Esther.

Stan drew a deep breath.

"That," be said softly, "I think it was sixty thousand million horsepower in a power beam. I think our friends the grid-makers have been working on armament to fight us with, and I think they've got something quite good! They don't like strangers. Torren was a stranger, and they got a shot at him, and they took it. Now they'll get set to come over here after us. If you'll excuse me, I'll go back to the drive."

He returned to the cabin where two out of a necessary eight graphite bars were in place. He worked. Fast. No man ever worked so fast or so fiercely or with such desperately steady hands. In twenty minutes he made the last, the final connection. Just as he dropped the hatch in place, Esther called anxiously:

"More machines coming, Stan! The microphones picked them up!"

"Coming!" he told her briskly. He went to the instrument board and threw switches here and there. "The normal thing," he said evenly, "would be to lift from the ground here, on landing drive, and go into field drive out of atmosphere. But we don't do it for two reasons. One is that we have no landing drive. The other is that at normal takeoff acceleration our friends of the grid would take a pot shot at us with the thing they used on Rob Torren. With sixty thousand million horsepower. So—here goes!"

He stabbed a simple push button.

With no perceptible interval and with no sensation of movement, the *Erebus* was out in deep space. The screens showed stars on every side—all the stars of the Galaxy. These were not the hostile, immobile, unfriendly stars the first voyagers of space had seen. With the Bowdoin-Hall field collapsing forty times a second, the stars moved visibly. The nearer ones moved more swiftly and the farther ones more slowly, but all moved. The cosmos seemed very small and almost cozy, and the stars mere fireflies and the Rim itself no more than a few miles away.

Stan watched. He said:

"We're not making much time. Not over six hundred lights, I'd say. But we'll get there."

"And—and when we do—"

"Hm," said Stan. "You can swear Torren said he'd committed the crimes he charged me with and faked the evidence against me. With that testimony, they'll examine the evidence as they do when there are no witnesses. It'll fall down. I'll be cleared."

"Stan!" said Esther indignantly. "I meant—"

"When I'm cleared," said Stan. "We'll get married."

"That," admitted Esther, "is what I had in mind."

He kissed her, and stood watching the moving cosmos critically.

"Our friends the grid-builders have gotten waked up now," he observed. "They know they're not the only intelligent race in the universe, and they may not like it. They're a fretful crew! But they'll have to be made friends with. And quick, or they might cause trouble. I think I'll apply to be assigned the task force that will undertake the job. It ought to be interesting! Not a dull moment!"

Esther scowled at him.

"Now," she protested, "you reduce me to being glad we're not making our proper speed! Because after you get back—"

"Listen, my dear," said Stan generously. "I'll promise to come home from time to time. And when I do I'll grab you like this, and kiss you like this—" There was an interlude. "And do you think you'll manage to survive!"

Esther gasped for breath. But she was smiling.

"I—I think I'll be able to stand it," she admitted.

"Good!" said Stan. "Now let's go have some breakfast!"

THE END

www.ingramcontent.com/pod-product-compliance
Lightning Source LLC
Chambersburg PA
CBHW050905120626
46554CB00003B/1030